Off the Pacific coast of Mexico, a whale is born in a sea of stars. Swimming with Mama Whale and surrounded by a protective pod, Baby Whale begins to grow and learn and soon comes to know all the ways of the whales and the sea.

Jonathan London's simple, poetic text captures the tenderness and drama in the life of the endangered sperm whale. And Jon Van Zyle's dynamic illustrations reveal the grace and magnificence of these mighty mammals.

"... a useful introduction to sperm whales." —*School Library Journal*

"... children will be caught up by the wonder of these magnificent behemoths."
—*Booklist*

For Gerard and Maureen, walkers watching —J. L.

To Victoria —J. V. Z.

First paperback edition published in 2007 by Chronicle Books LLC.

Text © 1999 by Jonathan London.
Illustrations © 1999 by Jon Van Zyle.

Book design by Paul Donald.
Typeset in ITC Bailey Sans.
The illustrations in this book were rendered in acrylic on masonite board.
Manufactured in China.
ISBN-10 0-8118-5761-1
ISBN-13 978-0-8118-5761-1

Library of Congress Cataloging-in-Publication data available.

Distributed in Canada by Raincoast Books
9050 Shaughnessy Street, Vancouver, British Columbia V6P 6E5

10 9 8 7 6 5 4 3 2 1

Chronicle Books LLC
680 Second Street, San Francisco, California 94107

www.chroniclekids.com

Baby Whale's Journey

by Jonathan London · illustrated by Jon Van Zyle

chronicle books · san francisco

Off the Pacific coast of Mexico,
on a warm April night,
two sperm whales circle each other.

They rub belly to belly,
lock jaws and nuzzle,
flippers touching
in a sea of stars.

Dawn comes,
  and the male, the "bull whale,"
swims away on his own —
    fifty tons sliding north
  toward Alaska.

Sixteen moons pass,
and the one
who stayed behind…

becomes two.

The new life
   slips smoothly
from the warmth
   of its mother's body
      into the coolness
      of the ocean.

And together,
   midwives and mother,
nudge Baby Whale
      to the surface
      for her very first breath.

Mama Whale
    pats her tenderly
    with her flipper,
and Baby Whale
    nuzzles for milk.

They are not aware
        that danger is near.

Killer whales are coming!

But when the orcas slice the surface,
Mama Whale spots them.
  And she and the others surround Baby Whale — tails in, heads out —
    until the orcas turn as one, away.

Now the sea calms,
      mirrors the sky.

Baby Whale follows her mother like a shadow,
          learning the rhythms of the sea.

They, too, roll north for the summers,
but not as far as the big lone males.
And always, always, they swim with the pod.

All the way,
    Mama Whale
speaks to her baby
    with creaks
    and clicks
        and murmurs.

Baby Whale clicks softly in return.

    She is never
        far behind
        when her mother
            swallows a seal
        or shark
            whole,
        or makes a meal
            of forty salmon.

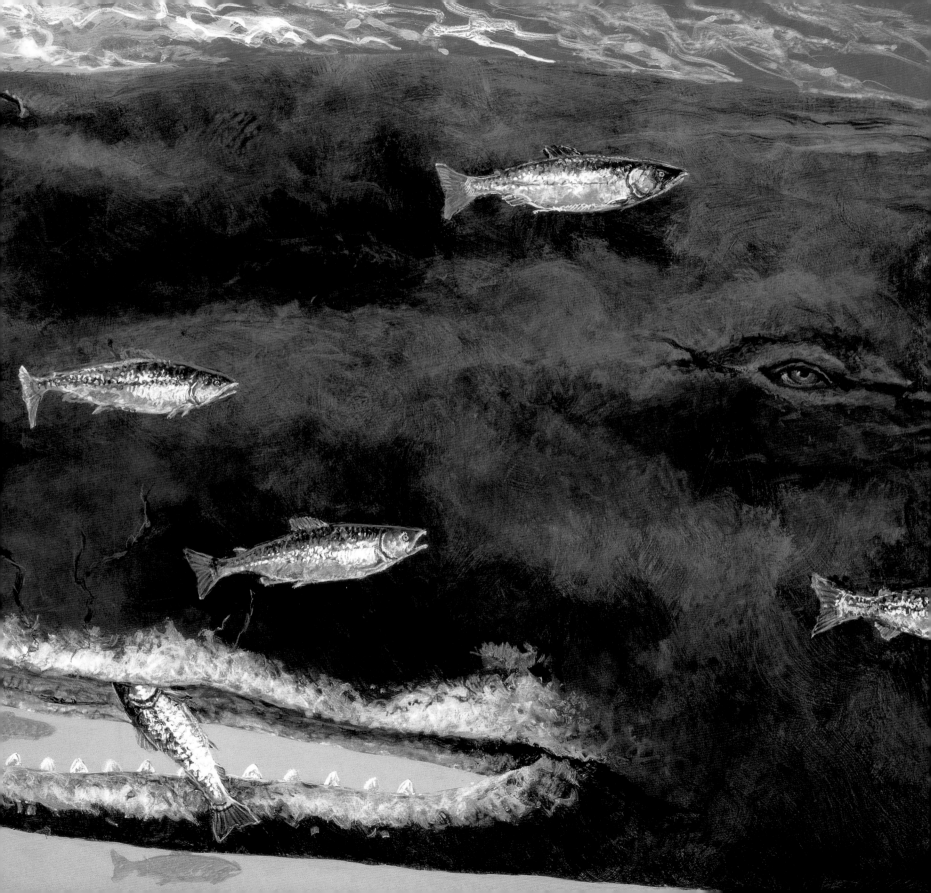

Baby Whale
  spends her days
    spy-hopping
      lob-tailing
        breaching

    then rolling over again
      to nurse at her mother's side.

Moons come, and moons go.
Baby Whale grows and grows.
She is learning the ways of the whales and the sea.

Nights, she floats at the surface under stars,
drifting in and out of sleep.
With each breath a small cloud blooms,
and disappears.

One evening, the full moon rising,
Baby Whale dives down and down with her mother
through green and purple twilight,
through swirling galaxies of luminous fish,
only to watch her vanish
into total blackness.

Baby Whale can hear her mother's clicks and murmurs fading.
Too deep.
Too deep.

She returns to the surface,
and waits.

Suddenly
the ocean erupts!

Mama Whale
bursts into the light of the moon.
The tentacles of
a sixty-foot-long giant squid
lace her body.

Baby Whale squeals
as her mother crashes back into the sea.
The giant squid writhes,
pumping ink
in rhythmic spurts.

Suckers grasp.
Tentacles twist.
And Mama Whale
rolls with them,
her huge teeth snapping.

At last, tentacles torn,
    the giant squid stops struggling.

Mama Whale has won.

Now Baby Whale feasts,
and the whole pod joins in —
the blue sea dancing
with whales and moonlight.

In the morning, Baby Whale —
    with her mother and the others —
swims toward the horizon.
        And together they leap, rise and blow
        like rolling shadows on the shining sea.

Afterword

Beneath the sea is another world, the world of the great whales. Like us, whales are mammals. They breathe air, have hair, give birth, and nurse their offspring. They are mammals in a sea of fish — beautiful, intelligent creatures in a world beneath the waves.

The sperm whales of this story are the largest toothed whales. (Some baleen whales, like the blue whale, are much bigger.) A full-grown male can grow up to 60 feet long (18 meters; about the length of a school bus!) and weigh 50 tons, while a female can grow to 40 feet (12 meters) and weigh 20 tons. Sperm whales have the largest brain of any animal — it weighs about 20 pounds (9 kilograms) — and they may be the most intelligent animal in the sea.

A newborn sperm whale weighs 1 ton and is 11 to 14 feet long (3 to 4 meters). A baby whale nurses as often as 40 times a day, drinking 2 or 3 gallons (8 to 12 liters) of rich milk at each nursing. In this way, a young calf may gain as much as 200 pounds (90 kilograms) in a day! After two years of nursing, young whales begin to catch their own food.

Sperm whales feed mainly on squid, but they also eat octopuses and fish. Young whales eat small squid near the water's surface, while their mothers dive deeper to feed. In fact, sperm whales are the best divers in the world. Male sperm whales have been known to dive to depths of over 10,000 feet and stay down for an hour and a half.

Down in these depths live giant squid. And "giant" is no exaggeration: a giant squid has tentacles 60 feet long (18 meters) and can weigh 1 to 2 tons. It has eyes the size of basketballs and a huge parrot-like beak. The beak and suction cups of giant squid leave scars on the sperm whales who battle them.

Female sperm whales and their young usually stay together in large groups—or pods—of 10 to 60 whales, while the grown males go off on their own. Like the males, females migrate north (south in the Southern Hemisphere), but prefer warmer waters. If they get separated, the clicking sounds they make can travel many miles through the water.

Sperm whales were listed as endangered in 1970 under the Endangered Species Conservation Act. Historically, the main threat to sperm whales was commercial whaling, which has since ceased. During the past two centuries, commercial whalers slaughtered one million sperm whales, mostly for their oil, which was used to light the lamps of the world.

Sperm whales swim in all the world's oceans, though they prefer deep waters. A sperm whale in the sea is a sight to behold. With its huge square head—about one third the length of its body—it is one of the most magnificent creatures ever to exist. To hear the clicks and murmurs of a mother and her baby is to experience a bond millions of years old.

A Chronicle Books Reader's Guide

Whether you are reading alone or sharing Baby Whale's Journey *with a group, this reader's guide can help you learn and discover the many layers of this book.*

BEFORE SHARING THIS BOOK

Ask readers to describe sperm whales. What does the front cover illustration reveal about sperm whales? **Invite** readers to listen and discover more about them.

Threat·ened (thrét-nd) *adj.* At risk of becoming endangered.

En·dan·gered (en-dáyn-jerd) *adj.* Faced with the danger of extinction.

Ex·tinct (ik-stíngkt) *adj.* No longer existing or living.

READING AND DISCUSSING

1. **Read** the text aloud, giving readers time to think about the language and study the illustrations.

2. **Read** the page that begins "Sixteen moons pass…" and **ask** readers what it means for a "moon to pass." **Discuss** why the author described time in that way.

3. **Explain** what a mammal is. **Ask** readers if they think a whale is a mammal or a fish. **Discuss** how the baby whale feeds after it is born.

4. Sperm whales are social creatures. They travel together in pods. **Ask** readers to describe how sperm whales communicate with each other. **Discuss** why it's important for them to communicate. **Ask** readers to point out examples in the story.

5. **Read** the afterword. **Discuss** how and why sperm whales have become an endangered species. What has changed to help sperm whales increase their population? **Discuss** things that could threaten them again and ways humans can help sperm whales.

AFTER READING THE BOOK

1. **Ask** readers why the author uses words like "sliding," "rolling," and "breaching" to describe the ways whales move in the sea. What do readers think terms like "spy-hopping," "lob-tailing," and "breaching" mean?

2. **Guide** readers in discovering objects that are the same in size as the whales featured in the story. **Encourage** them to create a chart or picture illustrating the size differences between sperm whales and other mammals like lions, elephants, and humans.

3. **Encourage** older readers to research and write to organizations to learn more about sperm whales.

4. **Suggest** readers visit the library to discover other books about endangered animals.

FACTS ABOUT SPERM WHALES

· Sperm whales need air to breathe but can hold their breath for more than an hour when diving for food.

· Sperm whales nurse their offspring as often as 40 times a day. After one or more years of nursing, young whales begin to catch their own food.

· Sperm whales usually rest vertically and lie motionless when sleeping. They sleep at different times of the day and night. They sleep with their eyes closed.

· Sperm whales live in groups, or pods, of 10–60 individuals. There is a lot of bodily contact between whales. They are very social creatures.

· Each pod of whales makes distinct "clicks" or sounds — possibly to keep the members of the pod together. They also communicate by slapping the water with their "flukes," or tails.

Jonathan London is the author of more than seventy books for children, including *The Eyes of Gray Wolf, Honey Paw and Lightfoot, Fire Race,* and *Hip Cat* (all published by Chronicle Books). He lives with his family in Northern California.

Jon Van Zyle is a successful artist and the illustrator of seventeen books for children, including *The Eyes of Gray Wolf, Honey Paw and Lightfoot,* and *Lewis and Papa: Adventure on the Santa Fe Trail* (all published by Chronicle Books). He and his wife Jona live with eighteen sled dogs in Alaska. To see his work, visit www.jonvanzyle.com.

ALSO BY JONATHAN LONDON AND JON VAN ZYLE:

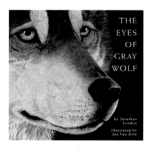

". . . a potent vision of a winter interlude as seen through the eyes of Gray Wolf." —★*Booklist,* starred review

"The author and artist . . . poetically and artistically portray a grizzly's birth and coming of age." —*Publishers Weekly*